For Aaron,
who knows lots already
about being BIG !

Kathy Stinson

© 1983 Kathy Stinson (text)
© 1983 Robin Baird Lewis (illustrations)

Annick Press Ltd. gratefully acknowledges the contributions of the Canada Council and the Ontario Arts Council.

Distributed in Canada and the USA by:
Firefly Books Ltd.
3520 Pharmacy Avenue, Unit 1-C
Scarborough, Ontario
M1W 2T8

Printed by Johanns Graphics Limited,
Waterloo, Ontario

Second printing, December 1983

Canadian Cataloguing in Publication Data
Stinson, Kathy.
  Big or little

(Annick toddler series)
ISBN 0-920236-30-8(bound).—ISBN 0-920236-32-4 (pbk.)

1. Lewis, Robin Baird. II. Title. III. Series

PS8587.T56B54 jC813'.54 C83-094034-0
PZ7.S74Bi

Big
or
Little?

Story
Kathy Stinson

Art
Robin Baird Lewis

ANNICK PRESS LTD., Toronto, Canada M2N 5S3

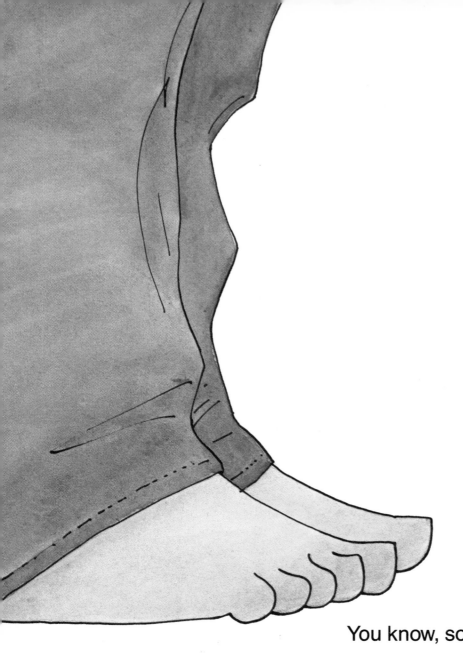

You know, sometimes I feel so big.

When I can tie my shoes,

and zip my jeans

and button my shirt all by myself,
that means I'm big.

But sometimes I feel so little.

When I can't   reach the button when I go and visit my friend,

that means I'm little.

When I remember to bring my library book back to nursery school because it's Tuesday,

that means I'm big.

When my mom yells at me 'cause
I can't find my other sock, again,

that means I'm little.

When I make my own breakfast
before anyone else gets up,

that means I'm big.

Once in a while I wake up and my
bed's wet, that means I'm little.

When I help take care of my little sister,
that means I'm big.

When I have to sit in the chair because
I forgot and rode my bike out into the street,

that means I'm little.

When somebody says, ''Thank you for holding the door, Matthew. That was very thoughtful,'' that means I'm big.

When I get lost between the bacon and the raisin bread, that means I'm little.

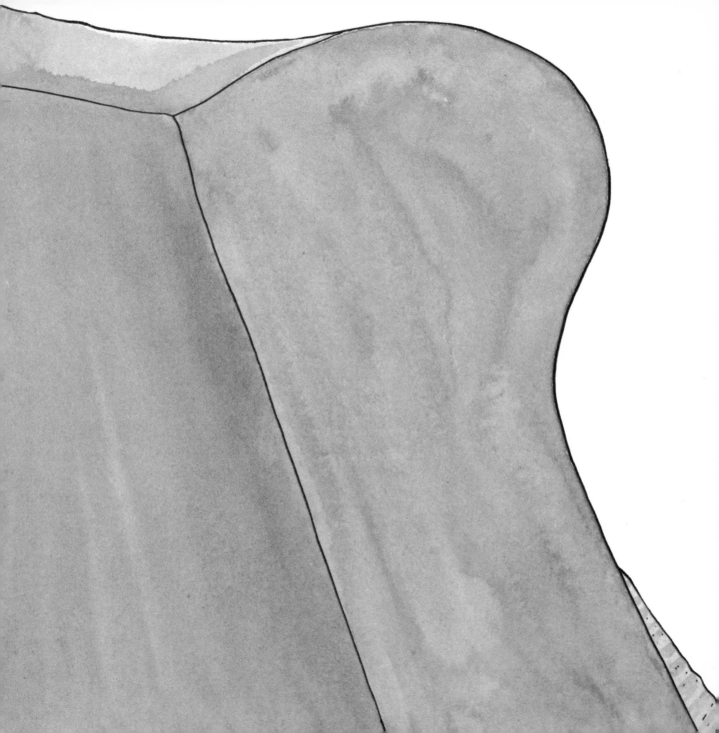

When my dad and I talk about space,
that means I'm big.

When my aunt buys me Bunny pyjamas,

that means I'm little.

But when the Bunny pyjamas don't come in my size,

that means I'm big.

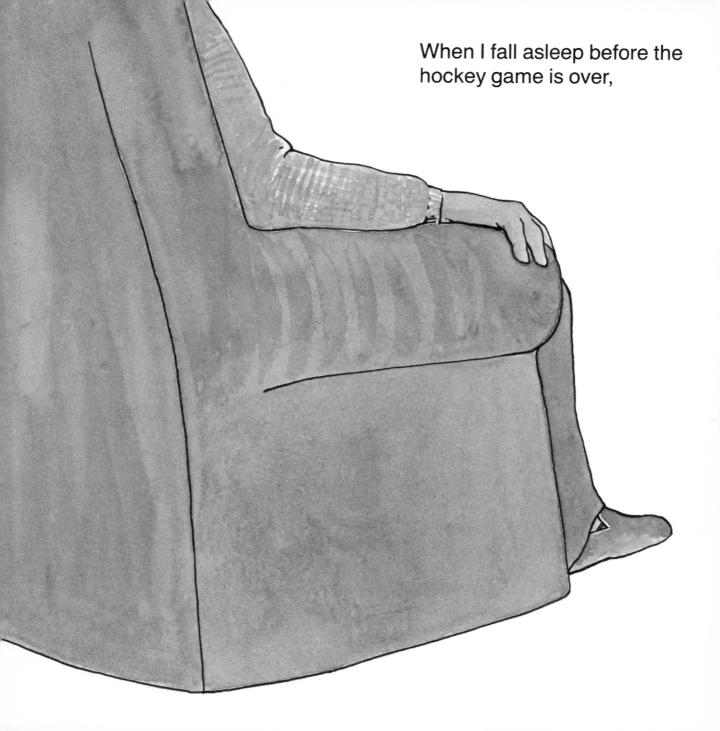

When I fall asleep before the hockey game is over,

that means I'm little.

Then my dad lifts me up in his big arms and carries me up to bed.

Mostly I want to be big,
but sometimes being little
is pretty good too.